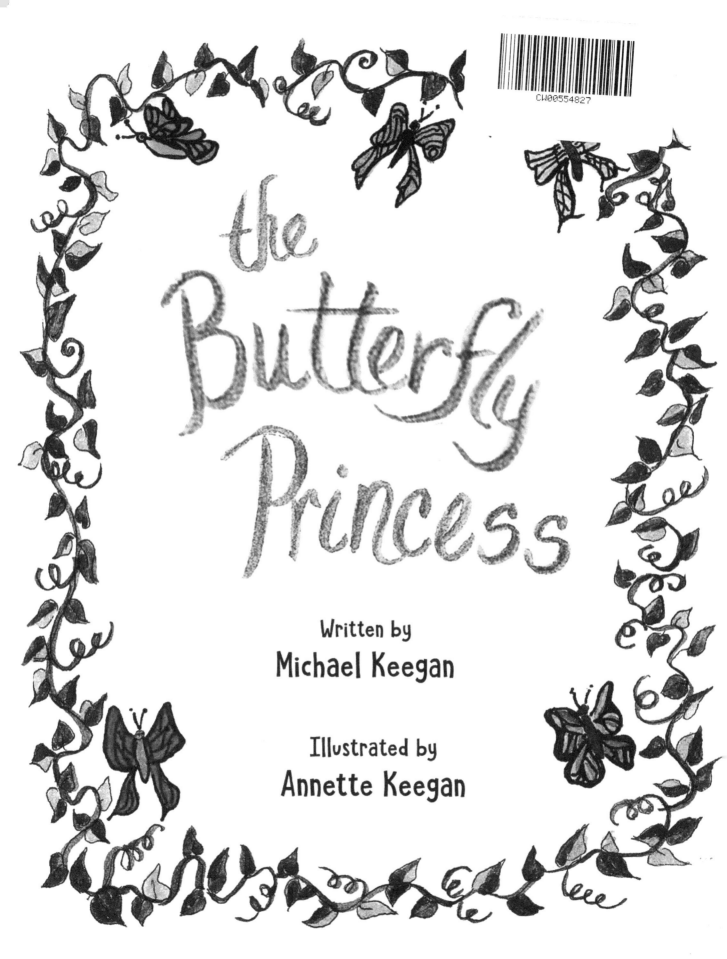

the Butterfly Princess

Written by
Michael Keegan

Illustrated by
Annette Keegan

Published in the United States by
Wild Mountain Press, Sonora, CA

Requests for permission to make copies of any part of this work should be submitted to puravida5@att.net.

Credits:

Artwork: Annette Keegan
Author Photo: Thad Waterbury

Cover Design and Interior Layout:
Melody Young,
(graphicdesignbymelody.blogspot.com)

ISBN-13: 978-0-578-73214-5

This story
is lovingly dedicated to our
Butterfly Princess . . .
Marley

and her beautiful mommy . . .
Kira

Oh . . . don't forget her brothers,
Jake and Bodie

Ya'll rock!!

Marley is a little girl who enjoys spending the day with her silly puppy Roxy.
They are adventurers who look for things
that grab their attention and give them reasons to play.

"Everyone is busy, busy," Marley says, "Mom and Dad said for me to get
outa the house and off my phone. What do you say Roxyroo?
Shall we look for a day of fun in the sun?
An adventure, some kind of story to tell them tonight
when we get home."

Roxy and Marley head out the door.

While walking Silly Roxy through the hard city streets,
Marley spies a beautiful butterfly.

Being the curious Princess she is, Marley bends to look at this butterfly.
It has beautiful colors and sits on a water fountain flapping its wings.
Marley moves closer and closer.
Butterfly does not move.
Does not fly.
Does not spook.

Marley is surprised to see a tear
in the butterfly's eye.

"Why do you cry?" asks Marley, "Can you not fly?"

"I have been fluttering alone and far from home," says Butterfly.
"If I fly, it is high in the sky to a place for princesses and puppies.

"I found this park because I heard a snappy bark.
When a Butterfly hears a bark, we seek it out.
We hope there is a princess and puppy
ready for an adventure."

Marley looks at Roxy, unsure what Butterfly means.

"Well, I am sorry to say, you beautiful butterfly, but you are far too small to carry my puppy and me," says Marley.

"Do not judge me by my size," Butterfly replies. "Our journey is drawn and my wings are strong."

"As I land on your finger," says Butterfly,
"grab your puppy and do not linger."

The wind is our guide,
        our power,
                our ride."

"We are given big strong wings because
we don't know if our princesses
will have one puppy or more.
With you and Roxy, I will be able to soar.

"I will open my wings and catch the wind," says Butterfly.
"I feel the gust,
I feel the blow."
The three lift up, up, up,
and away they go!

"Higher and higher into the sky!" Marley hollers.

Above the clouds they fly,
attached to their friend the butterfly,
riding the strength of its wings
with the flow of the wind.

"How high can you fly?" asks Marley.
"Are we going somewhere beautiful high in the sky?"

"To a cloud of beauty, a cloud under the sun,"
answers Butterfly with a gleam in its eye.
"The cloud in the sky where the butterflies,
princesses and puppies play,
for I am your guide, your chosen ride.
My job is to be with you, to stay by your side.
All little girls are born to be Princesses,
to find the Butterfly who will be their guide."

Ahead in the distance floats an enormous cloud.
Fluffy and white.
A magnificent vision.
A beautiful sight.
They fly toward the top of this
spectacular cloud
to the place where butterflies, princesses and puppies are allowed.

"Oh Butterfly, how strong you fly! Are you growing tired
from carrying Roxy and me?" asks Marley anxiously,
for she notices Butterfly growing more and more exhausted.

"I must try harder and harder,
and fly higher and higher," hollers Butterfly,
"for the other side of this cloud is the destiny we seek."

Butterfly uses all of its strength to hold on to Marley and Roxy
and fly over the fluffy peak.

"YOU CAN DO IT!" Marley yells.
"YOU CAN DO IT! We are a team, together in this endeavor.
We can do anything forever, together!"

Butterfly flaps her wings faster and faster,
harder and harder.

"We're almost there," Marley says excitedly. "It's not much farther!"

With an exhausted flap of its wings, Butterfly gasps,
"I need more strength to conquer this length."

A moment passes. Then suddenly at last,
a friend of this journey comes back with a blast!

A strong gust of wind lifts them higher and higher
above the cloud, high in the sky.

"Hoorah! Hooray!" cheers Marley.
"We made it over the cloud!"

She and Roxy look down amazed.

For within the cloud, they see a valley of green.
Through the haze of the cloud, it's hard to make out,
but from high in the sky, it looks like
the most beautiful green they have ever seen.

As they flutter down in the middle of the cloud,
they see a beautiful meadow
with rolling hills, flowers, and trees.
Through the middle of it all flows a river.
There are princesses and puppies dancing and playing
as their butterflies sit by and watch the joy they deliver.

"Now that we have arrived," says Butterfly,
"I must take some time to rest.
Look at all the princesses and puppies.
It is your time to do as you wish.
Kick your shoes off and let your feet feel the grass.
You are a Butterfly Princess and you are my guest."

Marley and Silly Roxy run across the meadow
and jump into the river.
Roxy grabs a stick wanting to fetch.
With the water splashing, they laugh and shiver.

Marley is happy to be in the cloud with the other princesses.
There are girls from far lands and farm lands.
        Girls from cities,
                from castles,
                        from cute tiny houses.
They wear their happiest clothes,
which speak of their excitement and display their flare.

Marley and Roxyroo were having so much fun
and meeting so many new friends.
The other princesses have silly puppies and many stories.
The excitement seems to have no end.

Marley meets their beautiful butterflies.
They are each different colors and all are beautiful and strong.
Everyone is so friendly they cannot help but feel they belong.

"To this cloud all the princesses of the world come," explained Butterfly,
"to talk and play to understand what happens from day to day.
It's time to discover exciting things and let your personality shine."

"Soon Princess Marley and Roxyroo,
we will have to get you home.
But we will stay a bit longer
to allow you to discover
who and what you may want to be,
and to enjoy making your
friendships stronger.

"Our job as butterflies is to beautify
the world and be your guides,"
says Butterfly with joy in its eyes.

After happy time passed,
Butterfly gathers Marley and Silly Roxy.

"Come now," Butterfly says. "I must take you home.
Give your friends hugs. Say your goodbyes.
It's time to flutter through skies
to your world
your city
your family."

Remember to look for Butterfly.
You may have to search in bushes,
around mountains, and across oceans,
but trust me, we will catch your eye.

You will never be alone.
Butterflies always appear to a princess seeking adventure.

Marely and Friends

Mike Keegan and Annette Keegan

Mike Keegan is my son. I am proud to say he is a Fire Captain/Paramedic working for an active Fire Department in the Bay Area of California, a U.S. Army Volunteer Cal Guard, and a wonderful father. The concept of his story came from a surfing trip he took to Costa Rica where butterflies abound. When his daughter was born, he created this sweet manuscript and asked me to illustrate it. We and our families live in the Sierra Foothill town of Sonora, California. I retired from Sonora High after teaching there for 16 years, and now I am a scenic artist for Sierra Repertory Theatre in Sonora.

I also love Butterflies...

Annette Keegan

Lightning Source UK Ltd.
Milton Keynes UK
UKHW050259150920
369869UK00009B/17